ICE BOY

David Ezra Stein

CANDLEWICK PRESS

Ice Boy had a normal life:

goofing around with his brothers and sisters . . .

dodging tough cubes from the back of the freezer.

Once in a while, someone was taken.

Usually for a person's drink.

To be chosen was the best thing
that could happen to an ice cube.

At least that's what Ice Boy's parents said.

But Ice Boy didn't want to be in a cold compress.

He wanted more.

So, even though Ice Boy's parents said,
"Never go outside. Never ever go outside,"

Ice Boy went outside.

And even though his doctor said,
"Never go in the sun. Never ever go in the sun,"
Ice Boy went in the sun.

In fact, he went to the beach.

Ice Boy went up to the edge
of the water and rolled right in.

His edges began to blur.

He was becoming . . .

Water Boy washed in with the tide.

The seashore was full of life.

Off a big swell, he soaked someone's towel.

He basked in the sun till he began to steam.

He was becoming . . .

Vapor Boy was light as air. He wafted so high,

he became a little drop.

He tap-danced on top of a thunderstorm . . .

until he froze and fell inside.

A big storm was no place for a little piece of ice.

ICE BOY again, whizzing through the sky in a summer hail.

Hey! I can see my house from here!

Then *oof!*—he hit the roof.
And *plink!*—he landed
in a drink.

And his parents were there!

"Ice Boy? Is that you?" they asked.
"Yes," said Ice Boy. "It *is* me!"

They floated together for a while.

"I'm sorry I ran away," said Ice Boy.
"I didn't want to be chosen."

Just then, the drink was lifted high in the air.

Luckily, the person tasted Ice Boy first.
"BLECCH!" he said. "This ice
tastes terrible."

We're free!

They landed in the grass.
"What will become of us?" said his parents.

"Let's find out," said Ice Boy.

Thanks to:

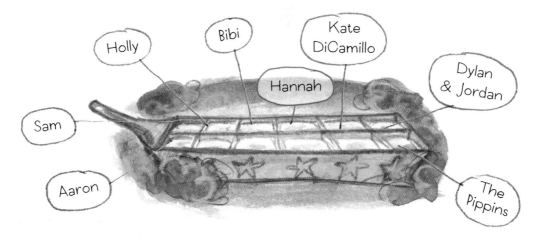

Holly

Bibi

Kate DiCamillo

Hannah

Dylan & Jordan

Sam

Aaron

The Pippins

You're pretty cool.

First paperback edition 2019

Library of Congress Catalog Card Number 2017933649
ISBN 978-0-7636-8203-3 (hardcover)
ISBN 978-1-5362-0893-1 (paperback)

19 20 21 22 23 24 CCP 10 9 8 7 6 5 4 3 2

Printed in Shenzhen, Guangdong, China

This book was typeset in Personal Manifesto Medium.
The illustrations were done in mixed media on watercolor paper.

Candlewick Press
99 Dover Street
Somerville, Massachusetts 02144

visit us at www.candlewick.com